The Girl and the Moon Rabbit

THIS BOOK BELONGS TO:

The Girl and the Moon Rabbit

Shada Elmansouri

Illustrated by
Luna Lag

The forest is filled with colourful flowers,
as Ningning plucks each to take home.

She jumps around across each rock, with a **big** colourful smile.

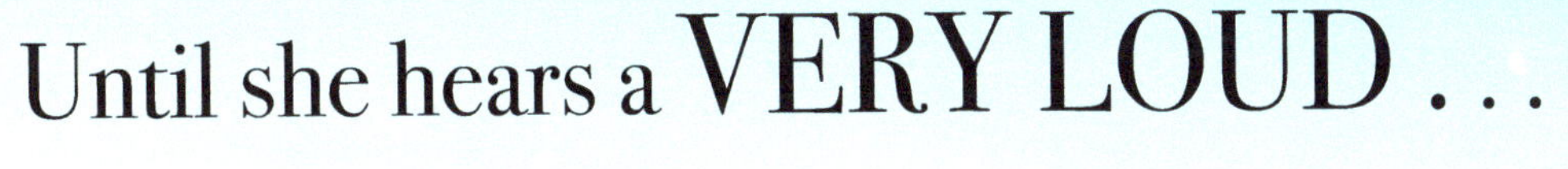
Until she hears a VERY LOUD . . .

THUMP!

She walks further into the forest,

and finds . . .

an **injured rabbit,**

with a scratch on his leg.

‘I will help you.’

Ningning picks up the rabbit,
and then takes him back to her home.

She gets a piece of cloth, and then rubs **medicine** on the rabbit's leg.

She asks the rabbit where he comes from.

He said, 'I come from up there!'

‘Woah!’

‘From the moon?’

Ningning is shocked,
but still wants to help out.

'From here, we can go up!'

Ningning says, as she makes a plan
to reach the moon.

She stretches . . . but it doesn't work.

She is **too short.**

Ningning asks for help.
Her animal friends are much **taller**
than Ningning,

but still can't reach
the moon.

Ningning is sad, so she goes home.

She asks her Nǎinai for help.

'Hmm?'

After dinner, they go outside.
Nǎinai tells Ningning to make a wish.

She hands her a bowl of water,
with the moon inside.

‘I wish my friend can go back home.’

Nothing happens.
Ningning is sad, so she goes to sleep.

The rabbit wakes up and nudges Ningning.

The moon is now shining so bright.

The rabbit is also shining with **magic**.
He is healed and has his powers back.

He thanks Ningning,
and gives her a gift of magical powers.

Ningning now stays with the moon rabbit, helping him take care of the moon.

THE END.

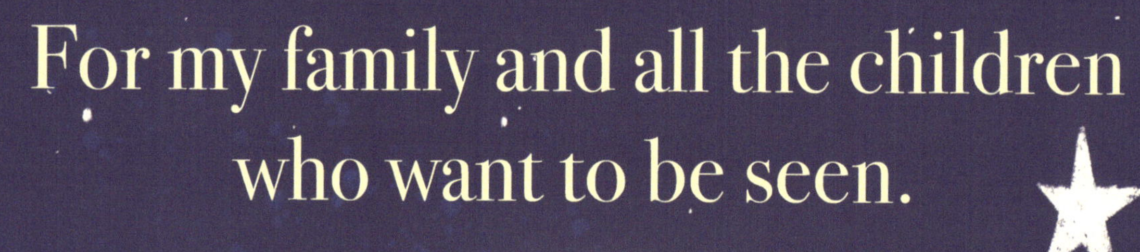

For my family and all the children who want to be seen.

A catalogue record for this book is available from the British Library.

ISBN 9798840156544

Typeset in Bodoni 72

www.ingramcontent.com/pod-product-compliance
Ingram Content Group UK Ltd.
Pitfield, Milton Keynes, MK11 3LW, UK
UKHW060117300726
14090UKWH00002B/235

* 9 7 9 8 8 4 0 1 5 6 5 4 4 *